# Pooks *and* Boots *Meet* Jesus

## JULIE K. WOOD

### Illustrated by Simon Good

ISBN 978-1-64003-710-6 (Paperback)
ISBN 978-1-64003-711-3 (Digital)

Covenant Books, Inc.
11661 Hwy 707
Murrells Inlet, SC 29576
www.covenantbooks.com

# Acknowledgement

My God, loving husband, Michael, and I would like to thank all those around the world who took the time to spread the word of God. I had this idea for the *Pooks, Boots, and Jesus* book series, and he smiled and gave me support, as he does with all my God-loving ideas! I love him and thank him for always supporting me and loving me as God loved the church. I am so blessed and thankful to him.

To my dear mother, Maria D. R. Kena, who literally gets on her knees in her neighborhood to pray with the children around her. She is a powerful prayer warrior from whom I have learned so much from. My mother took my faith to a new level. To my beloved sisters Daisy and Sable Kena. I thank them as well from my heart. Daisy has always been there for the family as my dad passed away when we were younger. She is the rock in our family. I also want to thank

Sable and her huge heart, for inspiring me to do this book. I am blessed to have such a wonderful husband and family.

We thank all the shelters, orphanages, ministries, and churches and individual missionaries around the world that help those in need, both body and soul. We also thank a ministry friend, Victoria Burch, who played an essential part in bringing this to reality. Along with her husband, Anthony, Victoria spent many years doing ministry work and raising ten wonderful children. Many more have entered into this labor, for which we are grateful.

We thank all those around the world who understand God's grace and mercy and believe they have a part to play. Our focus is helping children and animals in need and bringing the light of the Gospel to all. This work would not have been possible without Jesus and those who helped in a selfless manner.

God bless all those that made this possible.

Then the King will say to those on his right, "Come, you who are blessed by my Father, inherit the Kingdom prepared for you from the creation of the world. For I was hungry, and you fed me. I was thirsty, and you gave me a drink. I was a stranger, and you invited me into your home. I was naked, and you gave me clothing. I was sick, and you cared for me. I was in prison, and you visited me." Then these righteous ones will reply, "Lord, when did we ever see you hungry and feed you? Or thirsty and give you something to drink? Or a stranger and show you hospitality? Or naked and give you clothing? When did we ever see you sick or in prison and visit you?" And the King will say, "I tell you the truth, when you did it to one of the least of these my brothers and sisters you were doing it to me!"

—Matthew 25:34–40 (New Living Translation)

Once upon a time, there were two adorable kitties. One was all-black, and the other was black with little white paws. They were left in the wilderness with no family, no mommy, no daddy, and no friends! They didn't even have names. It was a cold, hard winter in the wilderness. They had no idea how to look for food, water, or shelter. They were in a mess—cold, tired, and hungry! All they wanted was food, and milk, and a soft place to lay their head at night. Seems like not much to ask, but it was.

But they had each other, these two little adorable kitties all by themselves in the wild!

They spent days and days looking around, high and low, for food and shelter. They found nothing but big trees, rocks, and icy snow crunching with every paw-step here alone in the wilderness.

After a tiresome sleep, the next morning they wandered a bit and found a tiny lake with plenty of water to drink (but, really, they would have loved some warm milk). They ran quickly to the lake and kept drinking until their little tummies were full of water. To their amazement, at that moment, they heard another little kitty crying for help!

They ran to the little kitty that was crying for help. They said, "What's wrong, little kitty?"

The little kitty told them that he was hurt. This kitty had a mixture of all kinds of color on the hair. They had never seen anything like him! He was caramel and vanilla and chocolate and licorice. All in one! He was adorable, but he was hurt, with lots of scratches and cuts all over him. They asked the hurt little kitty, "How did you get hurt?"

Little kitty said, "I've been in the cold wilderness for weeks. I'm so hungry. I'm so thirsty! I got cut trying to stay warm underneath the rocks and leaves and way up high in the trees, hiding as best I could." The little kitty had a broken leg from falling from one of the trees!

They felt so sad. They quickly found some rags, someone's old sweatshirt in the wilderness, and a piece of wood to wrap around the kitty's leg to help it heal. They washed the rags and used them to clean all the cuts on the kitten's body. They got some water from the lake and gave it to little kitty in need. They wondered, *What is little kitty's name?* They even found some grass underneath the snow, so they could feed the kitty in need. After furiously pawing away the snow, the smell and taste of tiny shoots of grass was quite delicious.

9

They decided to name the hurt little kitty Bandit. They named it Bandit because of the bandages around his broken leg. They continued to help little Bandit each day as he began to heal.

In a week or two, Bandit got so much better! One day as they were all playing in the wilderness and still very cold and hungry, they saw someone heading their way. It was a *big* someone, a big man. Should they be scared?

But the man was so nice; he grabbed all of them and put them inside a little box. At first, they were scared that he was going to do something bad, but he didn't. He put a blanket in there for them where they could all stay warm. They were giggling at how funny it felt to be bouncing in the box.

The man took them to a large building where there were many, many kitties and puppies. They were very quiet inside the box, just listening to all the people talk in this building. The man handed the box over to the lady in the building.

The lady opened the box and hugged them all, even kissed them on their furry foreheads. Then she cleaned them up and put them in their own little cages. For the first time in their lives, they had their own rooms! They had really needed a bath, and the lady kindly obliged. She brought bowls for each of them, one for milk and one for kitty tidbits. So delicious!

The kitties could not believe it! Their own cage, their own blanket, and it was nice and warm in the building. They looked around the building and saw so many puppies and kitties inside the other cages. *Will we ever get out?* they thought.

Many people came to the special building. They would pick out puppies and kitties to play with them. All the puppies and kitties were so happy to be around the people.

As the people played with all the puppies and kitties, some of them would go home with the families. They never came back to the building. Now they had their own families to take care of them.

Three little adorable kitties—the one that was all-black, the other one that was black and white, and the other one that had several colors—sat in the cage and watched all the other kitties and puppies go home with people. They were happy for the other pets but also sad that nobody wanted them.

But this one very special day, they saw a happy couple come into the building. The couple walked to their cage. And the lady who worked in the building pulled out the black kitty and the black-and-white kitty. The happy couple hugged and squeezed and played with the two adorable kitties. They decided to take the two adorable kitties to their happy warm home.

The two kitties got in a nice little cage and were put in the car. They all drove to their new happy warm home. But they thought, *Who will take care of Bandit?*

As the happy couple pulled them out of the car and took them into their home, they were so excited to see such a big home with lots of windows where they could see trees and birds and the beautiful blue sky.

25

They were so excited! They saw all their new toys and a warm bed for each of them to sleep in by the living room fireplace. The two adorable kitties began to chase each other around from room to room throughout the house. The house was huge and filled with so much love. Each room had so much furniture they could play on. Each room had big windows where they could see the trees and birds. They could not believe this was their home. The happy couple watched them run around and have fun. They were filled with joy seeing the kitties so happy. The happy couple got their dinner ready that night. They made them some nice warm chicken chunks and gravy with milk. What a meal! The two kitties could not believe this was their food, they never had anything this good before in their lives. They were so happy!

The happy couple then took the time to pray over the two adorable kitties and thanked Jesus for letting them find them. At that very moment, they named the all-black kitty Pooks, and the black-and-white kitty Boots.

Pooks and Boots were so happy to be home and they both had full tummies resting in front of a big warm fireplace.

But they couldn't help but think of Bandit and wonder if he had found a home just as nice. They remembered seeing Bandit all by himself in the cage as they left the building that day. Bandit looked so sad that they left the cage, but at the same time, he was happy they had found a home.

Pooks and Boots had a new mommy and daddy in their new home. They asked their new mommy and daddy who Jesus was because they always heard them praying to Jesus. They asked Mommy and Daddy, "Will Bandit be okay?"

Mommy and daddy said that Bandit would be just fine and find a home soon. They said they would pray to Jesus that Bandit found a home. That made them happy. Mommy and Daddy told Pooks and Boots that Jesus is amazing! They said, "Imagine every superhero you know. Jesus is better and bigger and more amazing than all the superheroes you know put together!"

They said Jesus can split the sea, Jesus can walk on water, Jesus can heal the sick, Jesus can heal the blind, and Jesus can heal those who can't walk. Jesus can do *anything!*

Pooks and Boots were so amazed about what they heard about Jesus. They asked, "Where is Jesus?"

Mommy and Daddy explained to them that Jesus made all of us. Jesus made Mommy and Daddy and all the kitties and puppies in the world. Jesus lives inside all those who love Him. Jesus lives inside of us, so He sees everything and hears our prayers all the time.

Mommy and Daddy told Pooks and Boots all they need to do is pray, and Jesus will be with them and help them in all things. Mommy and Daddy said whenever they get scared, all they need to do is pray to Jesus, and everything will be better.

A few days later, Mommy and Daddy left them in the house to go get more food. They were all by themselves in the house, and it began to storm outside! The thunderstorm shook the house. The rain was hitting the windows so hard.

Pooks and Boots got really scared and ran underneath the bed. But then they remembered what Mommy and Daddy said about praying to Jesus. So they started to pray to Jesus.

Suddenly, they heard a voice tell them, "Don't be afraid."

They said, "Who are you?"

The voice said, "You have seen and heard me before."

Pooks and Boots said, "We have never seen or heard you before."

The voice said, "You have seen and helped me. You helped me when I was tired, cold, hungry, and sick in the wilderness, and when I was in a cage in the shelter."

The voice answered it was Jesus, and the storm stopped. Even in their hearts, the storm of fear stopped! Pooks and Boots at that very moment remembered they had helped little Bandit in the wilderness and shelter.

Jesus told Pooks and Boots, "Always remember, whenever you take care of anyone in need, you are taking care of me!"

From this day forward, Pooks and Boots spend each day helping those in need. And they pray you do the same.

If you want to write to Pooks and Boots, please go to their website at pooksbootsandjesus.com. They really want to know all about you!

# Afterword

The story, *Pooks and Boots Meet Jesus* is told from the viewpoint of two real, live adorable cats named Pooks and Boots. Pages filled with words allow them to "talk" with children and parents so they hear the Word of God and by hearing, they learn. Too many voices today compete for attention and pull them away from what is good. This can be confusing for children. I created this book because of this reason—to bring the Gospel of Jesus into all homes in a fun and easy way to understand God's powerful and abundant love.

I remember being a child and had no clue who I was in Jesus and felt so lost and lonely. I want to give children the tools and resources I never had until I was an adult. I am praying that *Pooks, Boots, and Jesus* books can give the children these tools that will allow them to grow into a confident child of God.

Think about it. Can you imagine your child if they understood the fundamentals of these Bible verses below?

For God so loved the world, that he gave his only begotten Son, that whosoever believeth in him should not perish, but have everlasting life. (John 3:16, KJV)

Because he hath set his love upon me, therefore will I deliver him: I will set him on high, because he hath known my name. (Psalms 91:14, KJV)

Nor height, nor depth, nor any other creature, shall be able to separate us from the love of God, which is in Christ Jesus our Lord. (Romans 8:39, KJV)

Finally, my brethren, be strong in the Lord, and in the power of his might. Put on the whole armour of God, that ye may be able to stand against the wiles of the devil. For we wrestle not against flesh and blood, but against principalities, against powers, against the rulers of the darkness of this world, against spiritual wickedness in high places. Wherefore take unto you the whole armour of God, that ye may be able to withstand in the evil day, and having done all, to stand. Stand therefore, having your loins girt about with truth, and having on the breastplate of righteousness; And your feet shod with the preparation of the gospel of peace; Above all, taking the shield of faith, wherewith ye shall be able to quench all the fiery darts of the wicked. And take the helmet of salvation, and the sword of the Spirit, which is the word of God: Praying always with all prayer and supplication in the Spirit, and watching thereunto with all perseverance and supplication for all saints; And for me, that utterance may be given unto me, that I may open my mouth boldly, to make known the mystery of the gospel, For which I am an ambassador in bonds: that therein I may speak boldly, as I ought to speak. (Ephesians 6:10–20, KJV)

I picture children dreaming of superheroes that don't exist. Why don't we give them the tools to visualize that Jesus is much stronger and better than any superhero they know, and He is real and can live inside them?

Can you imagine your child getting up each morning saying, "I am saved, and protected. Nothing can separate me from Jesus, and I am wearing the armor of God!" and on top of that, they understood this concept?

Can you imagine how confident and loved they would feel? Let's face it: today's world brings so much negativity, which is why we need to arm our children with these superhero thoughts of Jesus that can live inside of them. That is what I pray my *Pooks, Boots, and Jesus* books will give children around the world.

The series *Pooks, Boots, and Jesus* is based upon the sure foundation of scripture. Each book begins with the scriptural reference from the Bible, which explains what the story will be based on. At all times, the beautiful thread of salvation by grace alone is woven throughout.

*Pooks and Boots Meet Jesus* explains the struggles they had in the wilderness but has a happy ending with a loving home.

Pooks and Boots know that they were saved from the cold wilderness by the hand of God, and now they spend the rest of their lives giving to children and animals in need with the Pooks, Boots, and Jesus Paw It Forward Program. This is their way of "pawing" it forward.

The *Pooks, Boots, and Jesus* team pray for all those who write to them. If your child or animal in need is selected,

Pooks and Boots may send money to their cause, or an autographed *Pooks, Boots and Jesus* book or maybe both. So reach out to them at their website: pooksbootsandjesus.com. They would love to hear from you!

Let us always remember the Bible verse Matthew 19:26 (KJV): "But Jesus beheld them, and said unto them, with men this is impossible; but with God all things are possible."

Julie K. Wood

CPSIA information can be obtained
at www.ICGtesting.com
Printed in the USA
BVHW02s1255280518
517560BV00024B/1585/P